Dinosaur vs.
THE POTTY

BOB SHEA

Disney • Hyperion Books/New York

For information address Disney·Hyperion Books,
114 Fifth Avenue, New York, New York 10011-5690.

First Edition
10 9 8 7 6 5 4 3 2 1
F850-6835-5-10166
Printed in Singapore

ISBN 978-1-4231-3339-1
Reinforced binding

Library of Congress Cataloging-in-Publication
Data on file.

Visit www.hyperionbooksforchildren.com

To Ryan for remembering to use the potty
and to Colleen for reminding him

DINOSAUR

WINS!

And doesn't need to use the potty!

roar! roar! roar!

Dinosaur versus...

splashing in the sprinkler!

roar!
roar!
roar!

DINOSAUR WINS!

And still doesn't need to use the potty!

roar! roar! roar!

Dinosaur versus...

a **three** juice box lunch!

And no, he doesn't need to use the potty!

Dinosaur versus...

watering his
pretend whale!

roar!

roar!

roar!

DINOSAUR
WINS AGAIN!

You'd think he'd need to use the potty!
But he says he doesn't!

roar! roar! roar!

Dinosaur versus...

splashing in rain puddles!

roar! roar! roar!

roar! roar! roar!

And does a victory dance!

Wait a second!
That's not a victory dance!

That looks like a . . .

POTTY DANCE!

Can he make it?

Can he get to the potty in time?

The potty wins!

Close one, Dinosaur! Real, real close.

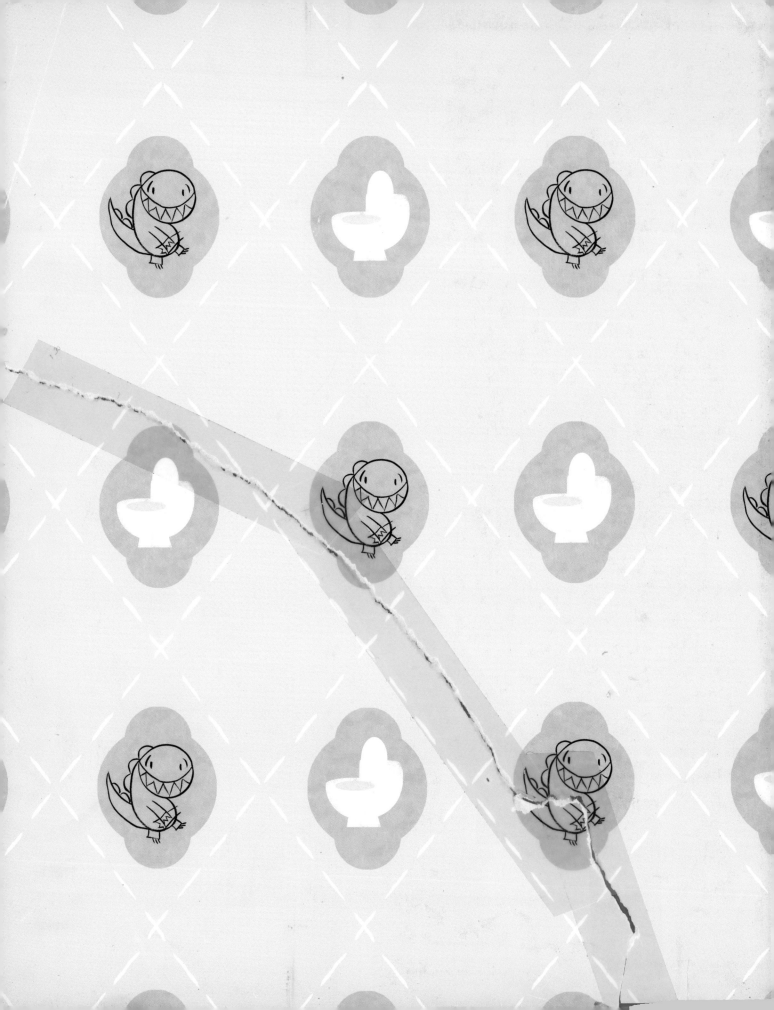